# A PAIR OF RED CLOGS

Illustrated by KAZUE MIZUMURA

# A Pair of Red Clogs

by MASAKO MATSUNO

PURPLE HOUSE PRESS

KENTUCKY

For my mother

Published by
Purple House Press
PO Box 787, Cynthiana, KY 41031

Publisher's Cataloging-in-Publication Data
Matsuno, Masako.
A pair of red clogs / by Masako Matsuno; illustrated by Kazue Mizumura.
p. cm.
Summary: After a young Japanese girl cracks her new red clogs playing the weather-telling game, she so longs for a new pair to replace them that she almost does a dishonest thing.
ISBN-10: 1-930900-20-1 and ISBN-13: 978-1-930900-20-2
[1. Japan — Fiction.   2. Values — Fiction.   3. Shoes — Fiction.] I. Mizumura, Kazue, ill. II. Title.
PZ7.M43155 Pai 2002   [E] — dc21   2002109525

Read more about our classic books for children at
www.PurpleHousePress.com

Printed in China
3  4  5  6  7  8  9  10

A pair of old cracked wooden clogs!
I found them last night in a storeroom of my house
when I was looking for a box to send a new pair of clogs
to my little granddaughter.

The new pair is painted with red lacquer,
and they shine beautifully.
The old pair is also painted with red lacquer,
and they, too, shone beautifully when they were new.
When the old pair was new,
I was as young as my granddaughter is now.

One evening,

when I was as young as my granddaughter is now,

I went shopping with my mother.

In the small town in the country where we lived, there were

many stores along the main street. At the end of the street,

there was a small tobacco shop with a red-painted postbox in front.

I loved to go into this shop, because wooden clogs were sold there, too.

I was going to choose a pair of them to wear to school

starting the next day.

Just one pair.

There were many clogs of many colors.

      A black pair,

          two blue pairs,

    three yellow pairs,

           four red pairs,

    five white pairs,

and many, many more than that.

All were ranged in order on wooden stands under the light.

Behind the stands, there were other shelves with other pairs of wooden clogs.

The blue would be nice when I wear my blue dress, I thought,

but the yellow ones would also be nice.

"Which pair would you like, little girl?" asked the lady of the store.

      Red?

  Blue?

        Yellow?

I wondered for a long while.

My mother was looking at me, smiling quietly.

I thought and thought, and finally decided to take the red ones.

They were painted with clear red lacquer,

and there was a thong of red and black on each clog.

It was almost dark when we went out of the shop

with the new clogs in my hands.

Lights were on in the stores,

and the goods of the stores looked very pretty under the lights.

Polished apples looked as if they were painted.

Fresh bluish fishes looked almost alive on blocks of shining ice,

and roses were still wearing dew on their dark red petals

as if they had just come from the gardens.

But my new clogs were the most beautiful of all!

They were so airy and so light
that I felt as if I was wearing nothing.
When I walked, they talked:

> KARA  KORO,  KARA  KORO.

When I ran, they sang:

> KORO  KORO,  KARA  KARA

along with me.
I went to school, I played with my friends,
I went shopping with my mother, wearing the new pair.
Everybody said, "Aren't they pretty!"
I was happy, very happy.

One evening when the sun was going down,

my friends and I were walking down the hill.

The sun was just setting, and everything looked orange in its rays,

the sky, the grasses, my friends, and I...

*"Ashita tenkini nare!"* one of the girls sang, and kicked

her wooden clogs into the air.

*"Ashita tenkini nare!"* (May it be fine tomorrow! it means.)

I did it too.

This game is called the weather-telling game,
and if your clogs fall to the ground like this,

it will be a fine day tomorrow.

And if like this,  there will be snow.

And if like this, it will rain.

And that is how I made a crack in my new clogs.

They did not talk:

> KARA KORO, KARA KORO, when I walked.

They did not sing:

> KORO KORO, KARA KARA, when I ran.

They just sounded:

> GARA GARA, GORO GORO.

I was...sad.

Shall I ask Mother to buy a new pair? I thought.

No, I knew she would not buy another pair so soon.

I remembered what she had told me when we bought them.

"Take good care of them," she had said. "Maybe I will buy another pair after a while, for the next festival day."

Oh, it was more than two months till then.

"She will not buy new ones yet," I said to myself.

So I kept on wearing them.

They were not new any more now that there was a crack in them.

Day by day, little by little, they got dirtier.

Do I have to wear them for another two months? I thought miserably.

I thought and thought…

                    and

                            I had a bright idea!

Suppose… Suppose this pair got very, very dirty; then

Mother could not help buying a new pair, because

she wouldn't like me to look dirty among the others.

Let's make this pair very dirty, I decided.

The very next day, on my way home from school,

I walked into a puddle to get the wooden clogs wet.

Then I went to a dusty field and shuffled my feet in the dirt.

Look what I was wearing! Just muddy pieces of wood!

"Now Mother must buy me a new pair," I said, "and they will sing

      KARA KORO, KARA KORO, when I walk,

      KORO KORO, KARA KARA, when I run.

People will say, 'Aren't they pretty?' again."

I was very pleased with my plan, and started toward home.


But while I was walking along, scuffing the dirty clogs,

I began to get uneasy. I began to be afraid that my mother would know

that I had made the clogs dirty on purpose.

      BETA BETA, BETA BETA,

the muddy pair seemed to murmur, as if they were saying,

      "You are a liar; you are telling a lie."

So,

I was walking slowly when I entered the kitchen where Mother was cooking.

"What's wrong with you, Mako?" she said, looking at my dirty feet.

"With whom were you playing? The boys? Is that brown stuff

just mud, or is it paint?"

"Just mud," I answered in a low voice.

"Go and wash your clogs quickly before the thongs turn brown. Then

squeeze the thongs softly, and wipe the water away with the old washcloth,

and put them near the bath-fire.

Not too near, otherwise the lacquer will come off," Mother said

in her usual soft voice.

I didn't move.

"What's the matter, Mako? Do it quickly, or they won't dry

before morning."

I, I could not say that the clogs were so dirty that I needed
a new pair.
Mother was not suspecting me at all.
And I remembered that you should try to clean a thing first before
you decide to buy a new one.
It was the way we always did.

So, I washed the clogs.
The mud came out easily because it had not yet had time to dry hard.
       Splash, splash, splash!
The water was cold, and
I was cold too.
I was sure that Mother would not buy me a new pair of clogs,
because the mud came out almost perfectly.

I squeezed the clog-thongs, and wiped the water away.

Then I put the clogs near the bath-fire, but not too near.

Now that they were clean again they looked quite pretty,

though there was still the crack.

And I saw that the black color of the thongs had come out and

dyed the red part.

All because they got wet!

"Come and eat, Mako, it's getting late," called Mother.

So I went and ate, leaving my wooden clogs, steaming a bit,

near the bath-fire in the kitchen.

"They will be dry soon," said Mother.

"Did you wash them by yourself, Mako?" asked Father.

"Good, very good."

"What did you play, Mako?" asked my brother curiously.

"I… I just played…" I answered in a little, little voice.

Now it was out of the question to ask for a new pair.

I felt very sad. I was ashamed of what I had done.

"Maybe I will buy a new pair before long," said Mother. "The crack makes too much noise when you run. But don't play the weather-telling game on the stone road, and be sure not to get wooden clogs wet too often. All right, Mako?"

"All right," I said, nodding.

Mother was smiling at me as usual, so

I tried to smile as usual, too,

but I couldn't.

I wanted to say something to her…

but I couldn't.

I just knew that I would never try to trick my mother again.

A long, long time has passed since then.

This pair of cracked clogs is almost as old as I am.

I am packing the new pair for my granddaughter.

Will she play the weather-telling game with this pair of clogs?

Will she kick them into the air and let them fall on the stone road?

Will she get them wet?

Yes, I think so, don't you?